THE JUMBLIES

THE JUMBLIES

Edward Lear

Illustrated by

Emily Bolam

ORCHARD BOOKS

Illustrations copyright © Emily Bolam 1992
First published in Great Britain in 1992 by
ORCHARD BOOKS
96 Leonard Street, London EC2A 4RH
Orchard Books Australia
14 Mars Road, Lane Cove, NSW 2066
The right of Emily Bolam to be identified as the illustrator of this work
has been asserted by her in accordance with the Copyright, Designs and Patents Act, 1988.
A CIP catalogue record for this book is available from the British Library.
1 85213 394 5
Printed in Belgium

They went to sea in a sieve, they did,
  In a sieve they went to sea;
In spite of all their friends could say,
On a winter's morn, on a stormy day,
  In a sieve they went to sea!

And when the sieve turned round and round,
And everyone cried, "You'll all be drowned!"
They called aloud, "Our sieve ain't big,
But we don't care a button! We don't care a fig!
In a sieve we'll go to sea!"

Far and few, far and few,
    Are the lands where the Jumblies live;
Their heads are green, and their hands are blue,
    And they went to sea in a sieve.

They sailed away in a sieve, they did,
   In a sieve they sailed so fast,
With only a beautiful pea-green veil
Tied with a riband by way of a sail,
   To a small tobacco-pipe mast;

And everyone said, who saw them go,
"O won't they be soon upset, you know!
For the sky is dark, and the voyage is long,
And happen what may, it's extremely wrong
    In a sieve to sail so fast!"

Far and few, far and few,
    Are the lands where the Jumblies live;

Their heads are green, and their hands are blue,
And they went to sea in a sieve.

The water it soon came in, it did,
  The water it soon came in;
So to keep them dry, they wrapped their feet
In a pinky paper all folded neat,
  And they fastened it down with a pin.

And they passed the night in a crockery-jar,
And each of them said, "How wise we are!
Though the sky be dark, and the voyage be long,
Yet we never can think we were rash or wrong,
 While round in our sieve we spin!"

Far and few, far and few,
    Are the lands where the Jumblies live;
Their heads are green, and their hands are blue,
    And they went to sea in a sieve.

And all night long they sailed away;
And when the sun went down,
They whistled and warbled a moony song
To the echoing sound of a coppery gong,
In the shade of the mountains brown.

"O Timballo! How happy we are,
When we live in a sieve and a crockery-jar,
And all night long in the moonlight pale,
We sail away with a pea-green sail,
In the shade of the mountains brown!"

Far and few, far and few,
    Are the lands where the Jumblies live;
Their heads are green, and their hands are blue,
    And they went to sea in a sieve.

They sailed to the Western Sea, they did,
To a land all covered with trees,

And they bought an owl,

and a useful cart,

USEFUL CART

And a pound of rice, and a cranberry tart,

CRAN-BERRY

RICE

And a hive of silvery bees.

And they bought a pig,

and some green jackdaws,
And a lovely monkey with lollipop paws,

And forty bottles of Ring-Bo-Ree,

And no end of Stilton cheese.

Far and few, far and few,
    Are the lands where the Jumblies live;
Their heads are green, and their hands are blue,
    And they went to sea in a sieve.

THE
WESTERN
SEA

N
W   E
S

CRUMPETTY TREE

THE VOYAG

THE LAKES

THE ZEMMERY FIDD

BONG TREES

LLY-BO-LEE

THE LAND COVERED WITH TREES

THE LANDS WHERE THE JUMBLIES LIVE

TORRIBLE ☠ ZONE

CHANKLY BORE

F THE JUMBLIES

And in twenty years they all came back,
In twenty years or more,

And everyone said, "How tall they've grown!
For they've been to the Lakes, and the Torrible Zone,
And the hills of the Chankly Bore";

And they drank their health, and gave them a feast
Of dumplings made of beautiful yeast;

And everyone said, "If we only live,
We too will go to sea in a sieve –
To the hills of the Chankly Bore!"

Far and few, far and few,
    Are the lands where the Jumblies live;
Their heads are green, and their hands are blue,
    And they went to sea in a sieve.